Fairytales Retold
The Death Of Koshchei
The Deathless

Fairytales Retold

The Death Of Koshchei The Deathless

Avril Sabine

Cracked Acorn Productions

Australia

Fairytales Retold
The Death Of Koshchei The Deathless

Published by

Cracked Acorn Productions

PO Box 1365

Gympie, Queensland 4570

Australia

978-1-925131-88-8 (Kindle)

978-1-925941-21-0 (EPUB)

978-1-925941-32-6 (Large Type Print)

Genre: Fairytales Retold Short Story

Cover design by Caitlyn Petersen

When Koshchei escapes, Prince Ivan has to find a way to outwit him or never see the one he loves again. How can he outwit a sorcerer who has managed to trick Baba Yaga, a witch so few have fooled?

*

People have been telling stories since the beginning of time. Fairytales, folklore, myths and legends are among some of the stories that have been told over and over through the centuries. The basic story remains the same, but each storyteller adds their own style, sometimes adding something unique to the tale.

*

This story was written by an Australian author using Australian spelling.

Chapter One: Ivan

Prince Ivan stood with his three sisters, Marya, Olga and Anna, watching as dirt fell upon their parents' coffins. When Olga dabbed at her eyes with a silk handkerchief, he couldn't help thinking about the conversation he'd had with his parents only months ago. At the time he'd tried to tell his father that there was no need to talk of death and what needed to be done once they were gone. It would be years before he would need to worry over such things.

Had they somehow known? He liked to think they hadn't. Liked to think it was his father being his usual organised self. The words rang in his mind, as if his father stood at his shoulder telling them to him again. 'When we have gone, don't keep your sisters by your side. Let them marry what suitors come wooing them. They will be fine. Let them marry who they choose as your mother and I did. As we are letting you do. Although we wouldn't mind if you were a little less slow in choosing your bride.'

Ivan started to smile at the memory of his father's chuckles, his mother reaching for her husband's hand with a fond smile. The fall of dirt drew him back to the present and the pain of his loss. There were moments when he couldn't believe they were no longer with them. He supposed it would take time.

Anna, the youngest, slipped her hand in his. "We should return home. There will be people wanting to pay their respects."

He nodded, leading the way to their carriage, polite nods for the condolences offered to them as they walked through those assembled. He handed his sisters into the carriage, joining them. They remained silent on the trip to their castle. He looked at Marya and Olga who sat across from him, their eyes red rimmed and Olga frequently using her handkerchief. Like him, they had their father's colouring of glossy brown hair and green eyes. When Anna made a noise, he turned to her, the only one who looked like their mother with her fair hair and pale blue eyes.

Anna again reached for his hand. "It's so difficult to believe."

He could only nod, lightly squeezing her hand.

They arrived home to numerous people wanting to offer sympathy and as the day dragged on, Ivan began to wish they would all go home. Gathering his sisters, he retreated to the gardens, asking the servants to encourage their guests to leave.

"If I have to say thank you to one more person, I might very well scream," Marya said.

Ivan smiled fleetingly. He could clearly imagine his sister doing exactly that. "Stroll through the gardens with me. Forget all of them for now."

Anna walked at his side. "I still can't believe they're gone."

There was nothing he could say so he remained silent. Although he supposed that was probably the best choice after all the endless conversations and condolences they'd endured. He guessed his sisters felt the same way as they remained silent too, walking with him through the gardens until the sky darkened and thunder rumbled in the distance.

Olga looked skywards. "Do you think they've all left?"

Ivan shrugged. "It doesn't matter. We need to return inside before this storm arrives."

Marya hurried along beside him. "It seems a fitting end to the day."

He couldn't argue that. Reaching

the castle, he held open the French doors, relieved to see only servants coming forward to see if they were in need of anything.

Thunder cracked overhead and Anna jumped slightly. "That sounded very close. We barely made it inside in time."

Ivan didn't have the chance to reply. There was another loud crack of thunder and the ceiling appeared to split open long enough for a falcon to fly into the room. The falcon landed on the floor, turning into a young man who bowed towards them.

Ivan nodded to the young man, a wizard who was a frequent visitor.

Falcon took a step towards Ivan. "I know most would think it an inappropriate time, but I have come to ask for Princess Marya's hand in marriage. It has been my intention for a while, but every time I plan to ask, something comes along to set my plans aside. Then I realised this wasn't something I should keep setting aside. It's far more important than all else as life can be unbearably short."

Ivan wanted to say no, that he'd buried his parents today and didn't want to lose his sister too. The word remained unspoken as his father's request once again sounded in his mind. "If my sister finds favour in your proposal I would not prevent a marriage between the two of you."

Falcon turned to Marya, taking her hand. Before he could say anything, Marya spoke. "Yes. Of course yes. I have waited months for you to ask me."

Ivan chuckled, surprised he was able to do so. But his sister's reply had been so typical of her that he hadn't been able to do otherwise. "Then I guess we have a wedding to plan."

The days passed quickly as wedding preparations went ahead, the ceremony eventually taking place. There were many tears when Marya said goodbye to her brother and sisters. Ivan, standing beside Olga and Anna, watched as the carriage bore Marya and her new husband to his palace.

The days continued to pass quickly and Ivan was kept busy running the kingdom, doing all the things his father had once done. It was almost a shock to find a year had gone by since their parents' passing and Ivan invited his two sisters to join him for a stroll in the gardens. Instead of silence they reminisced about other times. There were a few tears, but there was also laughter caused by some of the memories they shared.

Before they were ready to return inside, the wind picked up and lightning lit the darkening sky. Ivan grabbed his sisters' hands, dashing with them back to the castle. They had barely made it inside when the rain began and for a second the ceiling appeared to split open in a blaze of fire and an eagle flew through to land on the floor, turning into a young man.

Ivan greeted the wizard, who'd been a frequent visitor the past year, and the young man bowed low. "I would like to request your permission to ask Princess Olga for her hand in marriage."

The words brought back memories of his parents and Ivan smiled, turning to his sister. "It was our parents' wish that you should choose for yourself the man you would marry. If Eagle finds favour in your eyes I will not interfere with your choice." At her nod, he ushered Anna from the room, giving Olga and her suitor a few minutes of privacy.

When the door closed, Anna glanced at it before continuing to walk at Ivan's side. "I will miss her."

"She hasn't said yes, yet."

Anna grinned. "She will. He is all she's talked about for months."

"And you haven't spoken of your suitor?"

Anna laughed. "Maybe once or twice."

Ivan grinned, not bothering to correct his sister. It had been more than once or twice. Thinking they'd had enough time, he gestured for

Anna to head back to the room where Olga waited to tell them her news.

It was as Anna had predicted and the following months were filled with wedding preparations. Once again Ivan found himself watching as another of his sisters drove away in a carriage to start a new life at her husband's palace.

Anna slipped her hand into Ivan's. "Will you be lonely when it's only you?"

"How could I be lonely in a castle filled with people?" He forced a smile to his lips, not wanting to say something that would have Anna feeling like she should stay instead of living her own life when the time came.

And it did come, a year later when their stroll through the gardens was interrupted by an oncoming storm.

They rushed inside to see the ceiling split open long enough for a raven to fly through and land on the floor, turning into a young man who'd regularly visited in the past couple of years.

The wizard bowed. "Prince Ivan, today I come to you not as a guest, but as a suitor asking for the hand of your sister, Princess Anna."

Ivan smiled, glancing at his sister before he answered Raven. "I won't interfere with my sister's choice. If you've managed to gain her affections I'll allow her to marry you." He barely managed to keep his smile in place when his sister came forward to take the wizard's hands, repeating the word 'yes' several times.

It seemed like the wedding preparations for Anna passed far quicker than those of Marya and

Olga's and he was once again watching a carriage take one of his sisters away. The words Anna had spoken when Olga had married came to mind. He was lonely. Like he'd feared. Turning away, he trudged inside, happy for his sisters while at the same time wishing they'd not travelled so far away.

The following year passed slowly and Ivan decided that Falcon had been right. Life was often short and instead of spending his time missing his sisters he should visit them. He set about planning for the lengthy journey. Making certain everything was in order, he found a suitable regent to take care of things in his absence before he set out.

He headed in the direction of Marya's palace, taking with him all he thought he might need on his journey, as well as men to guard him against the thieves and rogues to be found on the roads. Several weeks into his journey, he came across a great plain littered with the dead from a battle.

It looked like none could be living, but he called out anyway. "If any man lives, answer me." He waited before calling out again.

A man moved, struggling to sit up.

Ivan dismounted and walked over to him. Crouching by his side, he saw the man wasn't far from death. "Can you tell me who won this battle?" He worried he might be riding into a war.

"The warrior, Princess Marya Morevna." He drew in a laboured breath. "She destroyed the army my lord sent against her, wanting to take her lands for himself." The man reached for Ivan. "Do you have water? I'm so thirsty."

Ivan called one of his men to fetch water. They were too late. The soldier was dead before he could be given a drink. Ivan rose to his feet, surveying the carnage, intrigued by the warrior princess who'd won against so large a host. He turned to his men. "Scout around. See if you can find where Princess Marya Morevna is now."

Chapter Two: Marya Morevna

Princess Marya Morevna sat in her tent, braiding her blond hair in preparation to chase after the stragglers from the army that had been sent against her. She'd ridden out to face them the moment news had been brought to her that they marched upon her castle.

"Your Royal Highness," her squire called from outside her tent.

Finished fixing her hair, she rose to her feet. "Enter."

The squire came in, letting the tent flap fall into place as he bowed. "There's a company of men headed towards our encampment."

"Help me with my armour then saddle my horse in case I should need it."

As soon as she'd donned her armour, she belted on her sword and strode outside to greet the man who'd reached her encampment. Around her she noticed her men were watching the newcomers, hands on sword hilts. She guessed, that like her, they were half expecting a trap. She stopped well away from the newcomers, watching as the leader swung out of the saddle, giving her a shallow bow.

"Are you the warrior, Princess Marya Morevna?"

She inclined her head. "Who might

you be?" She was intrigued by the handsome young man with the clear green eyes who had ridden into her encampment with so few men. He would soon learn his folly if he'd come with trickery in mind.

"Prince Ivan. I was on my way to visit my sister, Princess Marya, when I came across the battlefield. A dying soldier told me of your exploits."

She eyed him carefully, trying to tell if there was any hint of disapproval. She didn't know him well enough, but wouldn't mind getting to know him better. "If anyone takes up arms against me I will face them rather than hide behind the walls of my castle in the hope I can outlast them in a siege."

Ivan nodded. "My father always said it was better to face an enemy than to cower away in the hope he would grow bored."

Marya Morevna smiled. This prince might be worth getting to know. Far too many who had come calling upon her over the years had bored her within minutes of meeting them. "Can I offer you refreshments? Have you been travelling for long? And how far from here is your sister?"

Ivan thanked her for her offer and Marya Morevna waved one of her men forward to see to his horse and to organise refreshments for his soldiers. Another one of her men brought refreshments for her and Ivan, setting them out on the table under the shade of an open pavilion. They spent the morning talking and as the day grew late, she offered to let him stay the night in the safety of her encampment, warning him of the stragglers she had planned to chase down that day.

Ivan accepted, offering to help her go after the remnants of her enemy's army tomorrow. Marya Morevna accepted, curious to see how he handled himself with a sword and spent the rest of the afternoon and evening talking and laughing. It was with great reluctance she bid him goodnight, promising to take him with her on the morrow.

It took them a few days to find all the stragglers and Marya Morevna was impressed with not only Ivan's abilities with a sword, but the way he talked about his family and his faith in her own ability to fight. He seemed to be a man who would not bore her easily, nor curtail her own pursuits as she defended her castle and people.

She sat across the table from him in

the open pavilion, torches lit around it and candles on the table, night having long since fallen. "It's time for me to return to my castle. The army has been destroyed and the one who thought to come against me has run home in defeat."

"I'll be sorry to part ways with you. I haven't had such a pleasant time in ages."

She smiled, glad he felt that way. "Then come with me. Marry me and return to my castle with me. From what you've said your regent can more than take care of your own holdings without you there to watch over him."

Ivan reached for her hand, taking it in his as his lips curved into a smile. "I had thought it too soon to even suggest such a proposal. But I'd planned to call upon you after I visited with my sisters."

His words warmed her and she momentarily tightened her grip on his hand. "I can wait until you've visited your family." She was nothing if not patient. Many of her enemies had learned that the hard way. If she could outwait them, waiting for Ivan to return should be far easier.

"I prefer your plan to mine. I'd be honoured to return to your castle and marry you." He rose to his feet, keeping hold of her hand, raising her up to stand in front of him. "More than honoured." He brought her hand to his lips, kissing it.

She nodded once. "Good. It's settled then. We shall marry upon the return to my castle." Her lips curved into a smile. "I look forward to introducing you to my people. I'm sure they'll be as delighted with you as I am."

They continued to talk into the night, making plans for their future as they finished their meal. Upon hearing of the upcoming wedding, many of the soldiers came forward to offer their congratulations. Marya Morevna knew most of them by name, thanking them and introducing them to Ivan.

The following day the encampment was dismantled and they set out for Marya Morevna's lands. When they arrived her people greeted them. They were as delighted with Ivan as the princess was. The planning of the wedding went ahead and the land celebrated for days.

They'd been married for several months when skirmishes along one of the borders had Marya Morevna planning to go to war again. She sent for Ivan after thanking the soldier who'd brought her the news.

Ivan strode into the room, going straight to her side and greeting her with a kiss. "Is something wrong?"

"Yes." She explained about the news that had been brought to her. "As much as I'd love to have you ride at my side, I fear this could be a ploy to draw me away from my castle. Would you take care of my lands while I go to battle? My regent isn't anywhere near as capable as yours and I worry he'd let the castle fall into enemy hands."

"I'll take care of things while you're gone. You can trust me to look after your people."

She took hold of his hand, leading him through the castle. "You can go wherever you wish in the castle and continue to make yourself at home." She entered a room, stopping in front of a closet. "But whatever you do, never open this closet. Can you promise me that?"

Ivan faced her. "What is in it?"

Inside was an enemy she'd captured years ago, one who would not die, no matter what she did. "You are better off not knowing. Promise me you'll never open it."

Ivan barely glanced at the closet, his gaze fixed on Marya Morevna. "I'll take care of everything while you're gone. You take care of the enemy causing problems along the border and return home as soon as you can."

"Thank you." She tightened her grip on his hand. "It'll be a relief knowing the castle will be safe while I'm gone."

"Do you need help organising anything for your journey?"

"That would be nice." She started to leave the room with him, pausing in the doorway. "You go ahead and I'll join you shortly." When he left, with a smile and a nod, she closed the door and faced the closet. It had been a while since she'd opened it. Crossing the room, her gaze remained on the closet. Opening the door, she stared at the decrepit old man locked in place by twelve chains.

He was tall and bony, his hair a tangled mane around his narrow face. He glared at her from beneath craggy brows with unblinking eyes, a nose jutting out over a mouth filled with crooked teeth set in a scraggly, grey beard. She knew he was more than he appeared. During the years she'd held him captive, after he'd first taken her captive, she'd watched the sorcerer wither away. Being as he was a shapeshifter she didn't know if this was his natural form or the handsome, youthful appearance he'd had when she'd first met him. The other form he often took was that of a whirlwind. She'd experienced that one when he'd taken her to his castle, determined to have her for his own.

"I will escape from here one day. Then we'll see how you like being held against your will."

"As little as last time, which is why I'll never release you. Unless you wish to tell me where you've hidden the egg, Koshchei."

He answered with a snarl. Not that she'd expected anything else. Closing the door, she turned away, thinking of the people she had scouring the lands for the island where he'd hidden his soul. It was buried under an oak tree, hidden in a needle that was inside an egg, in a duck, inside a rabbit that was locked in an iron chest. And if the chest were found and opened, the rabbit would try to run away. If the rabbit was killed, the duck would flee. She'd explained all of this to those she'd sent out to find the egg. For with that egg, Koshchei could either be controlled or killed. The heart of his power and his life was inside the needle and if the egg broke, so would the needle. It would cause hundreds of years to descend upon him at once, killing him in an instant.

She'd learned the secret of his deathlessness by trickery. The sorcerer was vain and easily flattered with a tendency to brag about his many conquests and how cunning he was. He'd bragged to her about the spell and how powerful it was. At first she'd thought there might be a way to break it without the need of the egg. But as the years had passed, she'd begun to fear that only by finding the egg would she be able to vanquish her enemy. Putting Koshchei from her mind, she lengthened her stride, thinking instead of the upcoming battle. She'd soon teach those who were causing problems on the border that she wasn't to be trifled with.

Chapter Three: Ivan

Ivan tried not to look in the closet, but it preyed on his mind. What did she have hidden in there? Why couldn't she trust him with the secret when she entrusted her lands and people with him? Twice he found himself standing in front of the closet, about to open the door. And twice he forced himself to walk away. The third time he reached for the door, he was unable to prevent himself from opening it. She should have trusted him. Should have shared her secrets with him. Hadn't he told her everything?

His mouth gaping, he stared at the aged man chained in the closet.

"Help me. Please help me."

Ivan closed his mouth, trying to understand how Marya Morevna could have done such a thing to a frail, old man. His voice was feeble and his hair matted, his body little more than bones.

"Have pity upon me, young man. Marya Morevna has left me hanging here for ten years with nothing to eat or drink. I beg you to give me a drink. My throat is drier than a desert."

"Ten years?" How was it possible? He thought of his brothers-in-law. Was Marya Morevna a witch? He wouldn't have thought it of her. And if she was, why hadn't she told him?

"Please. Take pity on me. If you do nothing else, at least give me a drink. I am thirsty enough I could drink a bucket full of water and still want more."

He couldn't resist the old man's pleas any longer and went to fetch a bucket of water. He held it to the man's mouth, surprised when he drank all of it. "What is your name?"

"Koshchei. And yours?"

"Ivan. Why did my wife do this to you?"

"I am terribly thirsty. How can you expect me to talk when I'm parched? If you won't set me free the least you can do is bring me another bucket of water."

"More?" He eyed the frail man up and down. "You'll make yourself sick drinking so much water."

"Then so be it, but maybe then I'll

no longer be driven mad by how thirsty I am."

Ivan stared at Koshchei a moment longer before he nodded and went to fill the bucket once more. When he brought it back, Koshchei drank every drop and begged for more. Fearing the man might make himself sick, but giving in anyway, Ivan fetched a third bucket of water and held it to Koshchei's mouth so he could drink it.

When the empty bucket was placed on the floor Koshchei grinned, showing crooked teeth. "Now we'll see how Marya Morevna likes being held prisoner."

Before Ivan could ask what Koshchei meant, the frail man seemed to change before his eyes, becoming a young man, the chains snapping as his body filled out and lost its frail look.

Koshchei bounded across the room, stopping by a window he flung open. "You may have my thanks, but you will not have Marya Morevna. She is mine." Turning into a whirlwind, he tore out the window.

Ivan ran to the window and stared in the direction the whirlwind had taken. What had he done? Why hadn't he trusted her? Unable to see the whirlwind any longer, he turned away from the window, closing the closet door rather than leave it open and have the servants asking questions. Surely Marya Morevna would be able to beat Koshchei. She obviously had previously or he wouldn't have been chained up.

The rest of the day he tried to convince himself that his wife would defeat the sorcerer. She was a warrior. Famed for her skill in battle. His hopes were dashed when a messenger arrived with the news that Marya Morevna had been captured by a whirlwind and the army was leaderless.

Ivan collapsed onto the nearest chair. It didn't seem possible that a fearless warrior such as his wife could have been captured. Why hadn't he left the door closed? Why had he let his curiosity take control? And why had he given into Koshchei's pleas? He had to do something. He couldn't sit here while his wife was in the hands of the shapeshifter. Rising to his feet, he paced the floor, trying to decide what to do. Somehow he had to find her. But he couldn't leave her lands unprotected.

It took time, that he didn't want

to waste, to organise someone to lead her army to sort out the border problem and a regent to take care of the lands while he was gone. Not wanting to leave the castle with even less men to protect it, he set out alone to search for his wife.

He travelled for days and on the dawn of the third day he saw a palace beside which stood an oak tree where a falcon sat on a branch. The falcon flew down to land in front of him, turning into his brother-in-law.

"Ivan, why do you look so troubled? Come inside. Marya will be happy to see you and you can tell us what's wrong."

Ivan followed Falcon inside, pleased to see his sister who was full of questions. It took him some time to tell her everything that had happened and the moment he mentioned

Koshchei's name he saw a change in his brother-in-law's expression. "What do you know about him?"

"He's an evil sorcerer who so feared death that he created a powerful spell to avoid it."

Ivan listened as Falcon explained how Koshchei had hidden his soul and how many people had searched for it over the years due to the many wrongs Koshchei had committed against them. "Is there no way to defeat him?"

"I don't know. But stay with us a little while and I'll consult with other wizards and knowledgeable people."

Ivan reluctantly agreed, wanting to go after his wife, but not knowing how he could help her escape from Koshchei's clutches. He spent three days with his sister and her husband and by the end of that time he knew no more about Koshchei than he had the day he'd arrived. When he said he needed to leave, his sister clung to him.

"I fear I'll never see you again. Koshchei is a powerful sorcerer and you are but a prince," Marya said.

"I have no choice. It's my fault my wife was captured by him."

"Let him go." Falcon slid his arm around her waist. "I'd do the same were it you taken." He turned to Ivan. "You will likely be gone a long time. Leave your silver spoon with us that we might look at it and think of you while you're gone."

Marya nodded. "Yes, leave the spoon with us, Ivan. It'll be something for us to remember you by."

Ivan left the spoon with them and set out again on his journey. More days passed and on the dawn of the third day he saw a palace, grander than the one Marya lived in, beside which stood an oak tree where an eagle sat on a branch. The eagle flew down to land in front of him, turning into his brother-in-law.

"Welcome to my home, Ivan. Olga was saying only the other day how much she missed you and her sisters. She'll be pleased to see you."

Before Ivan could return the greeting, his sister came running outside, throwing her arms around him, seeming to cry, laugh and talk all at once. She drew him inside, telling him of all that had happened in her life, finally asking about himself.

Olga held tightly to Ivan's hand. "You must get your wife back. We'll do what we can to help."

Eagle nodded. "I'll ask all those I

know if they've heard where Koshchei can be found."

Ivan agreed to stay, but when three days had passed and Eagle was unable to find any new information, Ivan said it was time to leave. Olga pleaded with him to stay, telling him he had no idea where to go. Ivan shrugged. "That doesn't matter. I'll search the entire world if I have to."

"Leave us something for us to remember you by," Eagle said. "Leave your silver fork."

Olga dabbed at her eyes with a silk handkerchief. "It'll be little enough comfort. Make sure you come back to visit and bring your wife to meet us."

Ivan left the fork with them, assuring Olga that he'd be back, and set out again on his journey. More days passed and on the dawn of the third day he saw a palace grander than the ones Marya and Olga lived in. Beside it stood an oak tree where a raven sat on a branch. The raven flew down to land in front of him, turning into his brother-in-law.

Before Ivan could greet Raven, the man called out to Anna, who came running out of the palace. She berated him for not having visited sooner and told him of all that had happened as she took him inside and called for refreshments. When they were seated she asked about him and cried out when she learned what had happened to his wife.

"How terrible. If there's anything we can do to help, you have only to ask it of us," Anna said.

"I'll talk to those who might know more about Koshchei and see if any of them know where he can be found," Raven said.

Raven was gone for three days and when he returned he had no information that could help. Disheartened, Ivan bid them farewell, leaving his silver snuffbox behind, when they asked it of him, to remember him by.

Ivan travelled for three days, stumbling upon the castle where Marya Morevna was held. She came running out to greet him. "What are you doing here?"

He wrapped his arms around her. "I've come to take you home. Where is Koshchei?"

"He's out hunting."

Ivan drew away from his wife, looking her over. "I had expected you to be in chains."

"He knows there's no need for them. How could I outrun the wind? Or even if I could manage to do that, how could I outrun his horse which is faster than the wind itself?"

"Come home with me. We can escape on my horse."

Marya Morevna shook her head. "It's impossible to escape. Why did you have to open the closet?"

"I'm sorry. I've regretted it every moment since he escaped. I couldn't have imagined anything like this would ever have happened. Please come with me. Surely we can outrun him." It took some time to convince Marya Morevna to take a chance and Ivan rode towards home, his wife seated behind him.

They travelled all day and when the evening came, the sound of hooves striking the ground behind them had Ivan turning to see Koshchei moving, at an impossible speed, on a magnificent horse. The distance between them vanished and Koshchei rode in front, forcing them to stop.

"Did you really think to escape me so easily?" Koshchei demanded. "The moment my horse stumbled beneath me I knew something was wrong and it soon told me you had stolen Marya Morevna away from me. As my horse said to me, it would have been possible to sow wheat, wait till it grows, reap it, thresh it, grind it into flour, bake it into pies, eat them and still have time to catch you. How did you think you could outrun the wind let alone outrun my horse?"

Ivan doubted Koshchei could be that fast, so he ignored his bragging. "How could you think I would let you keep Marya Morevna captive and not try and rescue her?"

Koshchei pointed a finger at Ivan,

the nail long enough to be a claw. "This time I will forgive you in exchange for the favour you did me, in giving me water, when I asked it of you. I would even forgive you a second time so great was the favour. But a third time I would cut you into bits." He dragged Marya Morevna from Ivan's horse, tossing her behind him before he rode away.

Ivan didn't have time to turn his horse in the direction Koshchei had taken before they were out of sight. Hopelessness washed over him and he had no idea how he could outrun so fast a horse. What if he'd arrived the moment Koshchei had left, would that have given him enough of a head start to have escaped? Eventually he forced himself to return to Koshchei's castle, watching for when he left to go hunting. The moment the sorcerer was out of sight, Ivan looked for Marya Morevna.

"Why have you returned? Go home, Ivan. You heard him. He threatened to cut you into bits."

He took hold of her hands when she would have walked away. "How can I leave you here? Come home with me."

"We can't outrun him. Give me time and I'm sure I can outwit him again."

"What if you can't? Surely he'll be more wary a second time. He's not long left so that should give us enough time to get away from him. At least try and escape with me. Surely we can find a way to trap him once we return home."

Marya Morevna eventually gave in and the two of them rode for home. As evening approached, once again they heard Koshchei riding behind them. He overtook them, forcing them to a stop.

"I will let you go one last time for the favour you did me, but if you ever try and take Marya Morevna from me again I will cut you into small pieces." Koshchei snatched her from Ivan's horse and rode away before Ivan could turn in his direction.

Ivan stared off into the distance, neither Koshchei nor Marya Morevna were visible. Despair settled over him. How could he return to the castle without her? He clearly remembered how lonely he'd been with all his sisters wed and no one to share his days. No one else would do. He hadn't met another woman who could compare with Marya Morevna. Even if it meant his life, he couldn't stop trying to rescue her.

Chapter Four: Marya Morevna

Marya Morevna watched as Koshchei rode away for a day of hunting, wishing he'd keep riding and never come back. He'd been more wary this time and no matter how much she flattered him she couldn't get him to spill any of his secrets or be trapped into becoming her prisoner. She wouldn't give up. It would take more patience than last time, but it wasn't impossible. If she'd done it once then she was certain she could do it again.

And this time she'd make sure no one could let him escape.

"Marya Morevna!"

She turned to see Ivan running towards her. "What are you doing here? Are you mad? He will cut you into little pieces." When he reached her, she held him tightly, the thought of him being killed by Koshchei causing a sharp pain to rush through her. "Return home before he finds you and carries out his threat."

"Let him try. I won't desert you."

Seeing how determined he was, she decided to stop wasting time and leave with him in the hope that somehow they could reach safety before Koshchei could come after them. Seated behind Ivan, she clung to him, frequently looking over her shoulder. No one followed. They raced towards home, going nowhere near as fast as Koshchei's horse could move.

She kept telling herself that she should make Ivan return her to Koshchei, but she wanted to leave every bit as much as he wanted to help her escape. Surely they could find a way to outwit the sorcerer. She had done so before. Yet this time she hadn't been able to. How long would it take before he stopped being wary of her?

The day passed much quicker than she liked and as evening approached she heard the sound of hoof beats behind them. Glancing over her shoulder she saw Koshchei rode after them, a barrel strapped behind him, and tightened her grip around Ivan's waist. She'd half made up her mind to fling herself from the back of the horse in the hope that Koshchei would let Ivan keep riding, when he overtook them and brought his horse to a stop in front of them.

"I warned you." Koshchei dragged Ivan from his horse.

"No." Marya Morevna threw herself at the sorcerer, trying to pull him away from Ivan.

Koshchei flung her from him, chopping Ivan into little pieces. He took the timber barrel off the back of his horse and threw the pieces in it.

Marya Morevna stared at the barrel, shock and anger keeping her immobile. She couldn't believe Ivan was dead. Why hadn't she tried harder to convince him to go home without her?

Koshchei covered the barrel in pitch and lifted it onto his shoulder, turning into a whirlwind and catching up Marya Morevna as well.

He crossed the land, his horse galloping after him, coming to a stop at the ocean edge, the moon rising in the sky.

Marya Morevna fell onto the sand, scrambling to her feet when she saw him toss the barrel into the sea. "No. Bring him back. Please, bring him back."

Koshchei grinned, crooked teeth gleaming in the moonlight. "How many times did you answer my pleas when I was chained in your closet?"

She couldn't answer him. Not that it mattered. He already knew the answer.

Koshchei laughed, throwing his head back, the sound turning into that of the wind as he changed shape and scooped her up, rushing across the land to return home, his horse galloping after him.

Chapter Five: Ivan

Ivan staggered to his feet, stretching. "I was asleep?" He looked around in confusion, unable to figure out why he was on a beach, the ocean to his left, his three brothers-in-law facing him.

Eagle shook his head. "Koshchei cut you into pieces, put you in a barrel and flung you into the sea."

"How did you find me? Or even know I was in trouble?" Ivan asked.

"The silver objects you left with us

turned black and we set out to find you," Raven said.

"I pulled the barrel from the sea." Eagle pointed to the barrel lying on the sand not far from them.

"I fetched the Water of Life," Falcon said.

"And I brought back the Water of Death," Raven said.

"Your sisters told us to take you home where you'd be safe," Eagle said.

Ivan shook his head. He couldn't go home. Not yet. "Do you know what happened to Marya Morevna?"

"Koshchei took her back to his castle with him," Raven said.

"I have to go after her."

"We cannot save you a second time," Eagle said.

"No matter how much our wives plead," Falcon said. "It isn't possible."

"I can't leave her with Koshchei. Not only because it's my fault he captured her. Would any of you leave your wife with him?" Ivan watched as the three wizards shook their heads. "Then explain to my sisters that I can't go home. Not until I have Marya Morevna back. And once I do, I'll visit each of you."

"How did he manage to catch you?" Falcon asked.

Ivan explained all that had happened since he'd last seen them.

"Where did he get his horse from?" Eagle asked.

Ivan stared at his brother-in-law. "I don't know." But he'd soon find out. If he had a horse equally as fast then Koshchei wouldn't be able to catch them. "Thank you." He looked at each of the wizards. "And thank my sisters for sending you to help."

Eagle clapped him on the shoulder. "You're our brother too. We couldn't do anything less." Turning into an eagle, the wizard flew away.

"You will find Koshchei in that direction." The wizard turned into a falcon and flew off.

"We tied a horse to that tree over there for you." With a smile in farewell, he changed into a raven and flew away.

Ivan waited until his brothers-in-law were out of sight before he collected the horse and rode in the direction he'd been given. He now had a plan. Marya Morevna wouldn't be Koshchei's prisoner for much longer.

Chapter Six: Marya Morevna

Marya Morevna stood by the window and watched Koshchei ride away. Anger burned through her. If only he could be slain with a sword. Maybe she should have been the one to go searching for the egg that contained his soul instead of leaving it to a handful of her people. Why had she gone with Ivan? She'd known Koshchei was serious when he'd threatened to cut her husband into pieces. He never made threats he didn't plan to keep.

She'd spent every moment since Ivan had been killed trying to think of ways to avenge his death. Koshchei had spent those days bragging about what he'd done and gloating over her loss, his wariness towards her gone. She would be patient a little longer and when he no longer expected anything, she'd find a way to capture him once more. She would chain him with a hundred chains and cast him into the deepest dungeon and no one would see him ever again.

Unable to stay inside the prison of Koshchei's house, she wandered outside, nearly screaming when Ivan stepped out from the trees. "I'm sorry I couldn't save you. I don't blame you for returning to haunt me. Know that

I will do all in my power to see Koshchei punished for what he did."

Ivan grinned, coming forward to take her hands. "My brothers-in-law brought me back to life. Are these the hands of the dead?"

She stared at the hands holding hers. The warm hands that felt as solid and real as her own. Her gaze travelled up to meet his. "You're alive?" At his nod she flung herself at him, holding him tight. "You must return home. I won't watch as you're killed again."

"I need you to find out where Koshchei got his horse."

She drew away enough to be able to meet his gaze. "Are you mad? He'll kill you again. Be patient. One day I'll find a way to escape him." Even though Ivan was somehow alive

Koshchei would pay for what he'd done.

"Please Marya Morevna, you should know I won't go home. If you want me to have any chance of surviving against Koshchei find out where he got his horse."

Looking into his eyes she could see his determination. "I am a warrior. I don't need you to fight my battles for me."

Ivan smiled. "That's why I need your help. Obviously I can't beat him on my own. Find out the information for me. Together we'll outwit the sorcerer and return to our home."

She slowly nodded, his words making sense. "You won't go making half thought out plans. We'll figure out what to do and outwit him together."

"Yes."

"I'll ask him this evening when he returns from hunting. You must go. I don't want him to know you were here and be suspicious."

Ivan's arms tightened around her before he let go. "I'll hide in the forest and wait for you to find out the information."

She watched him leave, returning inside to wait for Koshchei. The day crept by and the sorcerer didn't arrive until evening. He strode inside, grinning. She kept her expression neutral when all she wanted to do was run him through with a sword. She lowered her gaze so he couldn't see the anger in her eyes. He bid her join him for a meal and during it he gloated over how he'd cut her husband into pieces and there was no way for her to escape him.

"If it hadn't been for your horse,

you would never have caught up with us. Who did you steal him from?" She made sure her voice was filled with bitterness.

Koshchei threw back his head and laughed. It took him nearly a minute before he could stop laughing to speak to her. "I didn't steal him. I worked three days for Baba Yaga. She lives beyond the thrice nine lands, in the thirtieth kingdom, on the other side of the fiery river. She has a mare she flies around the world on every day and many other mares nearly as good. I watched over her mares without losing a single one and in return she gave me a foal. Not theft, but there was some trickery. I wasn't about to let her get the better of me."

"How did you trick Baba Yaga?" She widened her eyes and tried to sound awed. It wasn't difficult after the rumours she'd heard about the witch.

"Who says it was me who did the trickery?" Koshchei asked slyly.

Knowing he'd become suspicious if she pushed him for an answer, she said. "Surely you exaggerate about needing to cross a fiery river. That wouldn't be possible."

Koshchei drew himself up to his full height. "You doubt I could manage?"

She shrugged. "I suppose if anyone could you might be able to." She spoke slowly and hesitantly, adding a touch of doubt to her voice.

Koshchei took a handkerchief from his pocket, holding it in his left hand, his right hand under it. "If I was to wave this three times over my palm a lofty bridge would spring up. With it I was able to cross the fiery river without getting singed."

She watched as he returned the handkerchief to his pocket. "It looks like an ordinary handkerchief to me."

"You think to trick me into using it in my home? Better than you have tried trickery and failed."

She listened to him brag about all the people who'd failed to trick him, trying to remain attentive. As the night dragged on she smothered a yawn and topped up his mug with more ale. Would he never go to sleep?

By the time Koshchei retired for the night, Marya Morevna had nearly fallen asleep herself. She struggled to remain awake so she could sneak into his bedchamber and steal the handkerchief. Several times she nodded off, jarring awake to check the time. When she finally stole the handkerchief, she hid it in the kitchen before retiring to her own bed, not wanting to risk having him find it on her. Throughout the rest of the night she slept fitfully, waking at every sound, half expecting Koshchei to drag her from sleep and demand where his handkerchief was. But he didn't and morning finally came. After he'd eaten his meal, he went out hunting.

The moment Koshchei was out of sight she grabbed the handkerchief from where she'd hidden it and raced into the forest. She nearly ran directly into Ivan, who stepped out from behind a tree. "I asked him about the information you wanted to know."

He held onto her as if afraid to let go. "What did he say?"

She held onto him equally as tight

as she told him everything she'd learned.

Keeping one arm wrapped around her, he took the handkerchief she held out. "Is this it? The one that creates bridges."

"Yes. You're going after one of the foals, aren't you?"

"It's our only chance."

She wished she could disagree. "Be careful. Baba Yaga is as tricky as Koshchei. Maybe more so. Take no chances and don't return here unless you have a horse that can outrun Koshchei's."

He kissed her before taking a step back, holding onto one of her hands. "I'll return for you as soon as it's possible."

She tightened her grip on his hand and for a moment feared she might not be able to let him go. Nodding, she forced her fingers to cooperate. "I'll be waiting for you." Turning away, she returned to Koshchei's castle. It was the last place she wanted to be, but until she had a way to outsmart him, there was no escape from Koshchei.

Chapter Seven: Ivan

Following Mayra Morevna's directions, Ivan reached the fiery river. Holding the handkerchief in his left hand he waved it over his right hand three times. A bridge sprang up across the fiery river, but the horse refused to carry him over it, terrified of the river below. After sending the horse home, he pocketed the handkerchief and crossed the fiery river without fear of being burnt. He glanced over his shoulder to see the horse was out of sight. Soon he would have a steed as marvellous as the one Koshchei owned. For now he would have to walk.

Leaving the bridge behind, he continued on to Baba Yaga's, wishing he'd thought to ask Marya Morevna for something to eat. There wasn't even a spring for him to drink from. He'd been so focused on helping her escape that he hadn't thought to tend to his own needs.

Coming across an outlandish bird and its young, Ivan said aloud, "I can eat one of those chickens."

"Please don't eat any of us," the largest outlandish bird said. "If you leave us be we would do you a good turn some time in the future."

He was surprised to hear it speak to him and didn't relish the thought of eating something that could talk.

"You're safe from me. You and your young."

"Thank you. One day I will return the favour."

His hunger growing worse, Ivan continued towards Baba Yaga's place. A little further along he saw a hive of bees in the forest. His stomach growled from hunger and he said aloud, "I could eat some honeycomb."

The queen bee flew out of the hive. "If you would leave my honey alone I would return the good deed one day in the future."

He stared at the bee, surprised to hear such a creature talking. Feeling terribly hungry, but unable to raid the hive of a talking bee, he said, "I'll leave your hive alone. You have nothing to fear from me." When the queen bee thanked him he continued on his way.

Exhausted, starving and starting to feel a little weak from hunger, he saw a lioness with her cub. Surely here was a creature he could eat. "I am hungry enough I could eat all of the cub and still want more."

"Please leave us alone," begged the lioness. "If you do us no harm, one day in the future I will do you a good turn."

He sighed heavily. It looked like in this part of the world he would be forced to go hungry. "You're safe from me." Weariness threaded through his tone and he forced himself to keep walking.

He could barely put one foot in front of the other he was so fatigued from hunger. Staring at the ground, watching where he placed his feet, he was nearly at Baba Yaga's house before he noticed it. Stopping, he stared at the house that had twelve poles set in the ground around it. On eleven of the poles was stuck a human head. The twelfth was empty. Involuntarily his hand went to his neck, rubbing it as if he could almost feel his head being cut off.

Taking a deep breath, he called out. "Hail, Granny."

Baba Yaga came out the front door. "Prince Ivan, what brings you to this part of the world?"

A chill ran through him at hearing his name on her lips. How had she known it? What trickery did the witch use to learn something he had never shared with her? He was tempted to flee, but the thought of Marya Morevna remaining a prisoner of Koshchei held him still. He drew in another deep breath. It helped as little as the first one. "I have come to earn a heroic steed from you."

Baba Yaga cackled. "Indeed, Prince Ivan. Well you won't have to work a year for me. A mere three days watching over my herds, without losing a single mare, will earn you one of my horses. Should you lose but one mare, your head will be impaled on that pole." She pointed to the twelfth one.

Still fighting the urge to flee, he met her gaze. "I thank you for the opportunity to own one of your magnificent horses."

She cackled again. "Come in and join me for supper and take your rest while you can. Tomorrow you'll be out with the sunrise watching over my herds until the end of the day."

He didn't hesitate. He would have eaten almost anything, unless of course it talked back to him. After supper he gratefully dropped onto the blankets she had set before the fire for him. Exhausted as he was, it took him ages to fall asleep. He couldn't stop thinking about Marya Morevna. How did she fare? His wife was also his first thought when he woke the next morning. Three days and he'd have a horse as fast as the one that Koshchei owned. The two of them would be able to escape on such a magical beast.

"Out of bed, Prince Ivan. There's food and drink on the table for you and then you can go about your business of minding my herds."

He thanked Baba Yaga for the food and as soon as he'd eaten, he drove the mares out into the field. They'd barely arrived when they tossed their heads and flicked their tails and took off in every direction. He didn't have the chance to move before they'd all disappeared from sight.

Ivan sank down onto the grass, despair washing over him. He'd been outwitted by Koshchei and now it looked like he'd also been outwitted by Baba Yaga. He dropped his head into his hands, closing his eyes. He had no idea what to do. The warmth of the day and the lack of sleep during the night caused him to drift off. He was woken near sunset by the outlandish bird.

"Wake up, Prince, the mares are all home."

Disorientated from sleep, he stared at the bird. "The mares? Home?"

"I have returned the favour you once did for me. We are now even." The bird flew away.

Ivan scrambled to his feet and

hurried back to Baba Yaga's house. Before he reached it, he heard her shrieking and hid so he could listen to what she had to say. He crept ever closer in the hope that he'd be able to see what was happening.

"What did you come home for?" Baba Yaga stomped around her mares, glaring at them.

"Birds came flying at us from every part of the world and nearly pecked our eyes out," one of the mares called out. There were numerous agreements from the rest of the herd.

"Tomorrow, don't go galloping across the open meadows, but hide in the thick forests where the birds can't follow."

The mares neighed in agreement.

Seeing Baba Yaga had calmed, Ivan returned to her house. "I've sent the mares home like you asked of me."

"I see that." Baba Yaga cackled. "And I will expect the same the next two days." When Ivan nodded she spoke again. "Come inside and join me for a meal and a rest before you begin work tomorrow."

Ivan followed her inside, joining her for a meal and lying down on the blankets that remained by the fire for him. Like the previous night he tossed and turned trying to sleep, worried about Marya Morevna. He had another two days to endure before he could help her escape Koshchei.

After breakfast the next morning, Baba Yaga said, "Mind you take good care of my mares. If you lose but one, your head will be stuck on that pole." She pointed to the empty pole.

"I'll return them before day's end, like I did yesterday." Now he knew what to expect, he was certain he could prevent them from running off. He drove them before him, herding them towards an area where he should be able to contain them. Before they reached it, they raced off in different directions, their heads high and their tails streaming behind them. They were gone so quickly he didn't have a chance to chase after them.

Ivan sank to the ground, burying his face in his hands. He'd been certain that this time he could have kept them from escaping. He had no idea what to do. He could only hope that somehow Marya Morevna would find her own way to outwit Koshchei, for it looked like he'd failed.

Falling asleep under the warmth of the sun, Ivan was woken by the lioness as the sun went down. He started at the creature, trying to figure out why she should wake him.

"Are you awake, Prince? I have sent the mares home to their mistress."

Ivan rose to his feet, hope beginning to return. "All of them?"

"Yes."

"Thank you, lioness."

She bowed her head. "Thank you for sparing my cub when you suffered great hunger. We are even, you and I."

Ivan nodded a single time, watching as the lioness bounded away. Once he was alone, he hurried back to Baba Yaga's house, hiding when he heard her berating her mares, creeping close so he could see what was happening.

"You stupid creatures. Why did

you return home? Did I not tell you to hide in the deep forest?"

They neighed, hanging their heads, one of them answering Baba Yaga. "Beasts of prey came running at us from all directions. If we hadn't fled from them they would have torn us to pieces."

"Tomorrow run to the sea. They won't follow you there."

Seeing Baba Yaga had calmed down, Ivan came out of hiding and joined her for the evening meal. Once it was eaten he lay down in front of the fire, but struggled to sleep after how long he'd slept that day.

The next morning Baba Yaga woke him, offered food and warned him of the consequences, pointing to the pole she would put his head on if he lost but one of her mares. She smiled when she pointed at the pole, as if she looked forward to the moment his head would be mounted on it.

"I won't lose any of them. Like the past two days they'll all return home." Knowing they planned to run towards the sea, he drove them in the opposite direction. It didn't help. They raced off, disappearing before he could do anything to catch them. He wandered around, trying to find them, but it was impossible. The sea was too far away and he could never reach it and return before the day ended. He sank to the ground covering his face with his hands as he thought of Marya Morevna. Would she miss him? She'd seemed relieved that his brothers-in-law had brought him back from the dead.

Still thinking of her, he fell asleep in the warm sunlight. A bee woke him as the sun set behind the forest. "Arise, Prince. The mares have been collected from the sea where they stood in the water up to their necks."

"Thank you. I'll return to Baba Yaga and ask for the foal she owes me."

"Do not trust her. Go to the stable and hide behind the mangers without letting her see you. There you will find a colt rolling in the muck. In the dead of night, when all is quiet, steal the colt and ride away from the house."

"Thank you for your advice."

"Thank you for not raiding my hive. I have returned the good deed you did me that day. Now we are even." The bee flew away, leaving Ivan to stare after her.

Not knowing if he should follow the bee's advice, Ivan decided to return to the house and see what kind of mood Baba Yaga was in. After all, the horses had been returned to her each evening and not a single creature had been lost.

Upon arriving back, he hid so he could watch as she berated the horses, shrieking at them for returning, demanding to know why they had.

"Swarms of bees flew at us from every direction, stinging us until we bled. We had no choice but to return."

Tonight Baba Yaga didn't calm, she continued to yell at the mares and threaten them, promising to put Ivan's head upon the pole for his trickery. He remained hidden, sneaking around to the stable as the bee had suggested and hiding behind the mangers. When Baba Yaga finally went to sleep, late that night, Ivan saddled a sorry looking colt and jumped on his back, galloping towards the fiery river.

The colt wasn't as fast as Koshchei's horse, but he crossed the land quick enough. They reached the river in no time and Ivan drew out the handkerchief, waving it across his right hand three times. A bridge sprang out of nowhere, spanning the river, and he was able to ride across. As sorry looking as it was, this horse had no fear of the fiery river.

The colt looked exhausted and half starved so Ivan let him graze in the meadow on the other side of the bridge in the hope it would give him the energy to continue. He stared at the bridge, wondering how to get rid of it. How long did it take to disappear? For all he knew it could have taken the entire time he'd been

at Baba Yaga's and she would be after
him once she realised he'd stolen one
of her horses.

Looking at the handkerchief, he
had the idea of waving it across his
left hand. The bridge narrowed. He
waved it once more and the bridge
became so narrow it was barely there.
About to wave it across his hand a
third time, to be rid of the bridge
completely, he stared at the fiery river
below. Hadn't Marya Morevna told
him to outwit Baba Yaga? He didn't
want the old woman chasing him
across the lands when he returned to
rescue his wife. One enemy was more
than enough.

He waited on the side of the bank
as the colt grazed, fattening before
his eyes, growing by the minute. By
the time Baba Yaga was riding across
the narrow bridge, threatening to

remove his head and place it on her pole, the sorry looking colt was now a fine steed, the equal of the one Koshchei owned. About to wave the handkerchief across his palm a third time, Ivan stared at the bridge as it broke in two, Baba Yaga plunging into the fiery river below. Running to the edge of the bank, he peered into the fiery river. There was no sign of Baba Yaga.

Ivan mounted his horse, urging it to return to Koshchei's castle. The beast sped across the land, faster than the wind, as fast as Koshchei's steed. They reached the forest near the sorcerer's castle and Ivan dismounted, trying to see who was at home. Not seeing Koshchei's horse, he came out of the forest, leading his own.

Marya Morevna burst out of the door, running towards him,

throwing her arms around him when she reached his side. "I feared you wouldn't survive an encounter with Baba Yaga. I have since heard stories of what she does to unsuspecting men. Does she really have their heads impaled on posts around her house?"

"I'll tell you all about it later. For now we must leave before Koshchei returns."

"Let us wait another day for surely he could be home at any minute."

Ivan patted the neck of his stallion. "I have a horse that's faster than the wind. He won't catch us. We'll leave today before anything else can happen." It took him several minutes to convince her and they'd no sooner mounted the horse and took to the forests than Koshchei chased after them.

Marya Morevna clung to Ivan.

"He'll cut you into little pieces if he catches you."

"He has to catch us first." Ivan urged his horse to keep going, but what he hadn't considered was that his horse carried two while Koshchei's carried but one.

Eventually Koshchei rode ahead, swinging down off his horse to stand in front of them, holding a large sword aloft. He drew his hand back to strike out at Ivan, but before he had the chance, the stallion reared up, striking at the sorcerer's skull with his hoof.

Ivan clung to the back of the stallion having nearly fallen off when the horse reared. He watched as Koshchei crumpled onto the ground. "He's dead?" Fearing the sorcerer was only stunned, Ivan leapt from the horse and grabbed a fallen tree branch and clubbed Koshchei over the head with it.

Marya Morevna slid off the stallion and ran forward to check the still figure. "I can't believe it. Koshchei the Deathless shouldn't be able to be killed by anything less than the destruction of his egg." She turned to look at the stallion. "Maybe a magical horse was the spell's weakness."

Ivan stared down at Koshchei. "Are you sure he's dead?" He thought of how he'd been brought back to life by his brothers-in-law. "What if the egg slowly heals him? After all, he hung in your closet for a decade with no food and water and that didn't kill him."

"Let's be certain of it." Marya began to gather timber. "We'll burn him on a pyre and scatter his ashes across the land. Even if the egg can somehow bring him back to life it would take decades or possibly centuries for it to do so."

Ivan joined her, piling branches around the body. Once the pyre was built, he set fire to it, watching as the flames consumed the body. "I still fear he'll return. Even with all of this."

Marya Morevna slipped her hand into his. "I'll continue to have people search for his egg. I'm sure one day it'll be found and then we'll know for certain he's dead and can never return to avenge himself on us."

When the fire burned out, they gathered the ashes and scattered them to the winds. They swirled away in all directions and Ivan dusted off his hands, mounting his stallion while Marya Morevna mounted Koshchei's horse.

She rode beside him. "Shall we return home?"

"Eventually. First I'd like you to meet my sisters and their husbands. Then we'll return home."

Marya smiled. "I'd like to meet your family after all I've heard about them." She urged the horse into a gallop. "And with how fast these beasts go we should arrive in no time."

Ivan kept pace with his wife, riding at her side as they crossed the country to visit the first of his sisters. They'd be pleased to see him and he wanted to let them know he was well, that both of them were, and to again thank his brothers-in-law for all they'd done. But he looked forward to returning home and spending time with Marya Morevna before his warrior princess headed off to her next battle. He looked towards her with a smile at the same moment as she looked at him.

"We outwitted him." Marya Morevna grinned.

He returned her grin. They had. And not only that, he'd defeated Baba Yaga. That was a tale he'd tell her later. When all the celebrating was done and they'd returned home. Between them they were able to outwit and defeat sorcerers and witches. He had no fear of what the future might bring. Whatever it was, they would face it and outwit it too.

Free Ebook

Subscribe to Avril's newsletter and receive a free ebook. This ebook is exclusive to those on her mailing list. To find out more about this offer visit:

www.avrilsabine.com/free-ebook

*

We value your privacy and will not sell, rent, exchange or loan your email address to third parties. Your information is confidential and you are under no obligation to remain on the mailing list and can unsubscribe at any time.

To The Reader

If you enjoyed this book, why not consider leaving a review to help other readers discover it too? Reader engagement is one of the few ways that lets an author know readers want more books in a particular series or genre. So leave a review and tell friends, not only about this book but also about other ones you've enjoyed, so you can continue to enjoy books by your favourite authors for years to come.

Dreams are meant to be lived,

Avril.

About The Author

Avril is an Australian author who lives with her family on acreage in South East Queensland. She writes mostly young adult and children's speculative fiction, but has been known to dabble in other genres. You can find more information about her at www.avrilsabine.com where you can also subscribe to her newsletter to be kept informed about new releases, current projects, blog posts and exclusive news.

Titles By Avril Sabine

Stories about strong characters and characters who discover their strengths.

SERIES

Assassins Of The Dead- Young Adult Fantasy/Paranormal

Book 1: Dark Blade

Book 2: Dragon Touched

Book 3: Society Against Vampires

Book 4: King's Request

Dragon Blood- Young Adult Urban Fantasy (with elements of romance)

(5 book series)

Book 1: Pliethin

Book 2: Wyvern

Book 3: Surety

Book 4: Knight

Book 5: Mage

Dragon Mage- Young Adult Urban Fantasy (with elements of romance)

(Series two of Dragon Blood series)

Book 1: Promise

Dragon Blood Chronicles- Young Adult Urban Fantasy (with elements of romance)

(Companion stand alone series to Dragon Blood)

Book 1: Oath

Book 2: Betrayed

Guardians Of The Round Table- Young Adult Fantasy LitRPG

(Co-written with Storm and Rhys Petersen)

Book 1: Dexterity Fail

Book 2: Goblin Boots

Book 3: Singed Feathers

Book 4: Frog Mage

Book 5: Crystal Mine

Book 6: Cursed Harp

Book 7: Treasure Seeker

Rosie's Rangers- Young Adult Western Steampunk

(6 book series)

Book 1: Justice

Book 2: Vengeance

Book 3: Treachery

Book 4: Accused

Book 5: Wanted

Book 6: Corruption

Mark Of Kings- Children's Fantasy

(Upper middle grade/preteen)

(4 book series)

Book 1: The Arena

Book 2: The Island

Book 3: The Assassin

Book 4: The King

STAND ALONE SERIES

Demon Hunters- Young Adult Urban Fantasy/Horror (with elements of romance)

Book 1: Blood Sacrifice

Book 2: Retribution

Book 3: Tainted

Book 4: Premonition

Book 5: Cursed

Book 6: Feud

Book 7: Extrication

Plea Of The Damned- Young Adult Urban Fantasy/Paranormal

(6 book series)

Book 1: Forgive Me Lucy

Book 2: Forgive Me Aiden

Book 3: Forgive Me Jena

Book 4: Forgive Me Kobe

Book 5: Forgive Me Marti

Book 6: Forgive Me Dawson

Realms Of The Fae- Young Adult Urban Fantasy (with elements of romance)

The Sword (short story in Like A Girl Anthology)

Heart Of Stone

Book 1: A Debt Owed

Book 2: Marked By The Hunt

Book 3: The Magic Collector

Book 4: An Unexpected Betrayal

Book 5: Imprisoned By Iron

Fairytales Retold (Short Stories)

Snow-White And Rose-Red

The Twelve Brothers

The Light Princess

Beauty And The Beast

Sleeping Beauty

Aschenputtel

The Golden Bird

The Frog Prince

The Death Of Koshchei The Deathless

Myths And Legends Retold (Short Stories)

Ion, Son Of Apollo

Sir Gawain And The Maid With The Narrow Sleeves

Princess Ilse, The Giant's Daughter

YOUNG ADULT NOVELS

Young Adult Fantasy (with elements of romance)

Elf Sight

Earth Bound

Young Adult Urban Fantasy

Stone Warrior (with elements of romance)

The Jungle Inside

Young Adult Contemporary (with elements of romance)

Through Your Eyes

The Ugly Stepsister

Perfect Little Princess

Young Adult Contemporary/ Paranormal

Whispers In The Dark (with elements of romance and same sex relationships)

Over Too Soon (with elements of romance)

Young Adult Sci-Fi

Experiment X-One-Six (Urban Sci-Fi/Superheroes)

An Endless Dawn (Post Apocalyptic Sci-Fi)

CHILDREN'S BOOKS

Dragon Lord (Preteen/early teens) (Fantasy)

The Irish Wizard (Upper middle grade) (Urban Fantasy)

SHORT STORIES

Urban Fantasy

Eternally Late

Dealings With Joe

Glimpses (short story in That Moment When Anthology)

Contemporary

The Brat Next Door

Fantasy LitRPG

(Set in the same world as Guardians Of The Round Table Series)

Tales Of Inadon 1: The Disc (Co-written with Storm and Rhys Petersen) (short story in Game On! Anthology)

Post Apocalyptic Sci-Fi

Compulsive Directive

NONFICTION

A Year Of Weekly Writing Exercises (Creative Writing)

Cooking For Families With Allergies (Cooking) (Co-written with Storm Petersen)

Tell Me A Story, Grandma (Memoir)

For the most up to date details on available titles visit:

www.avrilsabine.com/books/bibliography

Disclaimer

This is a work of fiction. Names, characters, businesses, places, events and incidents are either the products of the author's imagination or used in a fictitious manner. Any resemblance to actual persons, living or dead, or actual events is purely coincidental. The opinions expressed or beliefs held are those of the characters and should not be assumed to be the opinions or beliefs of the author.